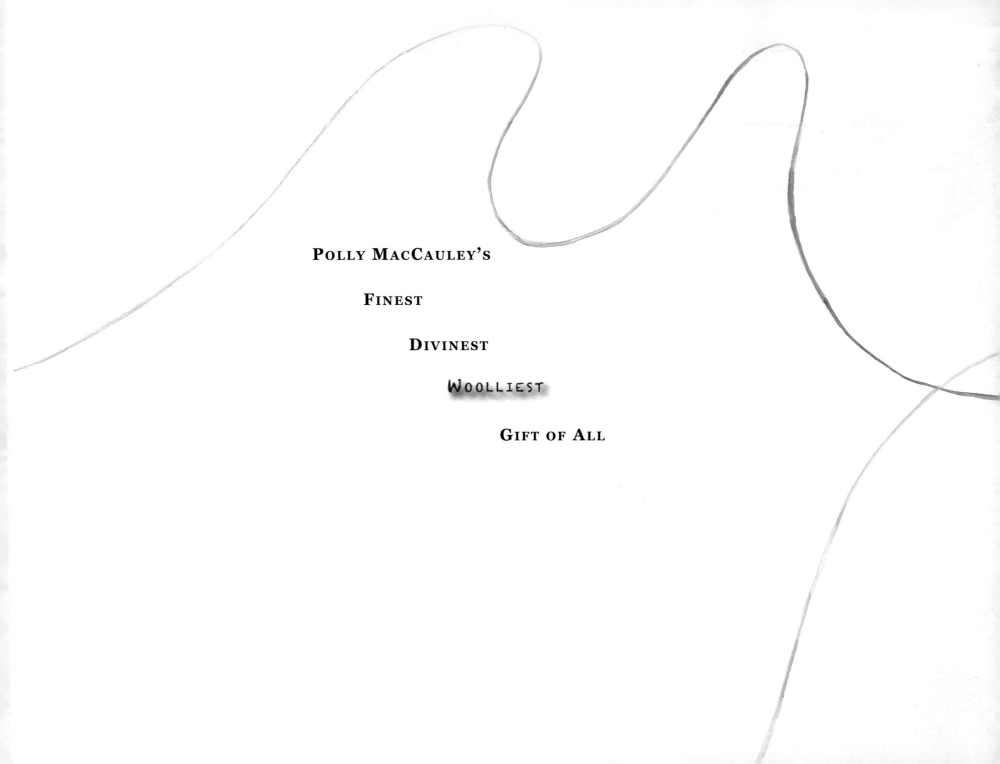

POLLY MacCAULEY'S

FINEST

DIVINEST

WOOLLIEST

GIFT OF ALL

POLLY MACCAULEY'S
FINEST
DIVINEST
WOOLLIEST
GIFT OF ALL

A Yarn for All Ages
by SHEREE FITCH

With Illustrations
by DARKA ERDELJI

Baaaaa

For Gillian, John, Katy, and Rory Crawford of Lismore Sheep Farm
in River John, where this idea was born many years ago

and for Deanne Fitzpatrick, artist and friend, whose creative spirit
inspires so many to create beauty every day
~ S. F.

For Miki
~ D. E.

To Listeners Young and Old

Tales are for telling and the truth may be tall,
My yarn is for spinning as the earth spins for all.

This is a yarn for
   a windy night
         or a rainy day
              or any old time
                   or a circle of souls
                        or a broken lonely heart—

so hunker down by a crackling fire and read aloud just to yourself
or share my yarn with those you love.

Not so very long ago from now
in a sweet-smelling barn
beside a red-roofed house
in the village of River John

A BABY LAMB WAS BORN.

Baaa! she bleated, the way baby lambs do—
a sound almost like a HUMAN BEING baby,
a real baby like I was or maybe even y-o-u.

I kid you not.

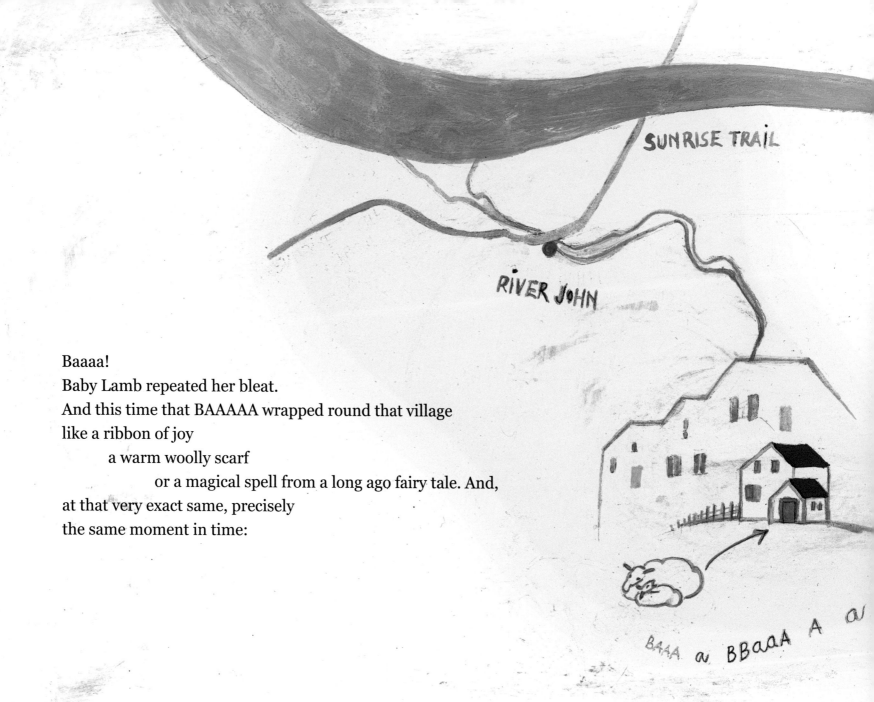

SUNRISE TRAIL

RIVER JOHN

Baaaa!
Baby Lamb repeated her bleat.
And this time that BAAAAA wrapped round that village
like a ribbon of joy
      a warm woolly scarf
           or a magical spell from a long ago fairy tale. And,
at that very exact same, precisely
the same moment in time:

BAAA a BBaaA A a

the farmers were plowing
the fisherfolk fishing
the fiddlers were fiddling
the bakers were baking
the makers were making

the preachers were praying
the readers were reading
the children were playing
the hens were laying
the gardeners were sowing
the carpenters sawing
the chickadees chirping
the babies were burping
the crows were cawing
the roosters were crowing
the mowers were mowing
the green grass was growing
and .....

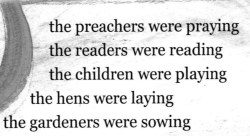

u BAAA a a a BAAAAA BAAAa a Baa a BAAA a B@aaa

an uncommonly lovely
lucky lilac-
      lavender
           breeze
              was *blooooow*-ing over
meandering meadows
& emerald-green fields
& a sea so blue it crinkled like foil &
sparkled so bright in the noon-day sun
it seemed as if stars had fallen from the sky and
tap-danced on the waves
before they lapped onto shore
with a sound like *woossshup,*
                 wassshup,
     wassup.
                     What's up?

Something special was up; something very special was rising on the Sunrise Trail:

a a BA BA Baa a a a A A BA BA a a a ba a a a

Even with all that
discombobulating bobble,
      that rambunctious riot
the burble and yapple   the buzz and the whirr
the worry and stir   the clatter and clang
the busyness and buzz   the workaday din of morning,
      everyone *everyone* **everyone**
in the village of River John and way beyond
      heard those
            first few
                  little
                        itty bitty
                        BAAAAAAAAAaas!

Out on the ocean, this caused a commotion.
A lobster fisherman looked up from hauling his traps.
"Well, ship ahoy and blow me down—what a joyful noise!"
he said as he reached for a lobster.

The lobster clapped its claws in applause. It did!
It snapped and trapped the finger of the fisherman—
"Ow", said the fisherman. "Ow yeow ow!"
He jumped up and down, and he spun round and round, and he stirred the water into
a whirlpool of waves.

So from the very beginning that innocent baby lamb really rocked
the boat.

Now, I wouldn't pull the wool over your eyes. Or Would I?

Far away in the small countship of Woolland, young Count Woolliam and his sister Woolamina, the Countess of Fleece and Fluff, were busy counting their fulsome flocks of slickly sheared sheep.

Not because they were trying to go to sleep, either.

In fact, counting their flocks kept them awake! They counted their sheep all day, and they counted them all night. They counted them at breakfast, and during four o'clock tea; they counted them while they played hopscotch and ping pong, and while they danced the highland fling. They counted them while they read. They even counted them in the bath! They were afraid they would never have enough wool for their woolly county.

They used fleece to line their velvet robes, wool for their finest sweaters and socks and scarves and mittens. They had different coloured felted hats for every day of the year. Count Woolliam and the Countess of Fleece and Fluff stacked woollen blankets on their bouncy beds, and decorated every wall in their estate with woven tapestries and rugs hooked with priceless wool. It was rumoured that all the toilets on the estate, even the ones in the outhouses, were lined with fleece, and soft on their noble posteriors.

What's more, a special blend of woollen fibres went into the making of the softest tissue for wiping their noble noses and ...
let's just leave it at that, shall we?

WOOL
WOOL
WOOL and WOOL

14

But outside the estate, in the village of Woolland, shearers and carders and spinners and weavers and knitters and felters and hookers worked hard every day. They were often hungry and cold, and so tired some even fell asleep at their spinning wheels. This caused quite a tangle by times. But did that matter to the greedy, needy count and countess who kept most of those woolly treasures for themselves? Not one bit.

"Where's my new hat? Another warm blanket—with three blue stripes on the left and ten on the right. And where's my sheepskin underwearrrrrrr???!!"

all wool

BAAA
BAAa
A
BaaaB
BAAaAaa a BBAAa BAA A Aaaa

When the count and countess heard the bleating of that baby lamb, they rubbed their mittened hands together, they jumped up and down on their woolly beds, in their fancy woolly pyjamas, and they hugged each other.

"It's come! It's come!" they cried. "The lamb we have awaited so long has arrived! Soon we will have wool to last forever! We must set out at once to discover where this lamb has been born!"

So they boarded the *Spinn-aker*, their sailboat, with a few of their own sheep, and set off.

Meanwhile, back in River John, down on the corner of the Sunrise Trail and the Cape John Road, the men who sat around the picnic table every day outside of Yap's, sat around the picnic table and yappety yapped.

WOOLLAND

"Hear that?" asked one

"Sure did," said another.

"Now, that's a baa you hear only once in lifetime," wheezed one old geezer.

"Something's going on in River John!" said his buddy named Buddy.

"Yup. Yup. Yup!" said the rest in unison.

Then all together, as if they'd practiced, they took long thoughtful sips of coffee.

For a few minutes it was all *Yup, Yhhhhup, Yhhhup* down at Yap's.

"M-m-mmmaybe P-p-p-pPolly M-m-mMacCauley's at the end of her…um, her um, s-s-s-s-special yarn," Buddy sputtered. His lips were trembling: he had spoken the UNSPOKENABLE unspeakable name and the unspokenable UNSPEAKABLE secret.

So the men sat, considering, silently, the unspeakable, the unspokenable, the improbable Polly MacCauley.

Now Polly MacCauley lived in a house at the edge of the village in the middle of the woods.

"Idiosyncratic," some said. "Right different, all right," said others—as if being different
was not a good thing.

BUT no one really knew her. Oh, they'd heard whispers, but they didn't know her sadness.
They didn't know her loneliness.

Strange as she may have seemed to many, Polly MacCauley was actually a very ordinary
woman—a very ordinary woman who did extra-ordinary, wild, and wondrous things with
W-O-O-L.

She hooked. She knitted.
She felted. She wove.

Sometimes she decorated the branches of trees with her woolly creations. "Just because I love to create something beautiful every day," she said to the hummingbirds.

Sometimes she knit mittens and sweaters and hats and blankets for people who had none. "Just because I love to create something useful every day," she said to the honeybees.

"Useful things are beautiful and beautiful things are useful," thrummed the hummingbirds to the bees and buzzed the bees to the hummingbirds.

"Indeed," the butterflies agreed. "Indeed."

Some called Polly MacCauley a witch, and some called her wise,
and because she was so rarely seen, some even called her a figment
of everyone else's imagination. But there were some who believed that
she sheared and spun and carded and dyed special wool from a special lamb
born long ago, and that she was the maker of many gifts.

"Who leaves all these colourfully crocheted hummingbirds,
neatly knitted butterflies and fabulously felted pixies—or are they
angels?—in the branches of trees and in secret places all over
the village," the children of River John asked their parents.

"Surely, it's the work of Polly MacCauley,"
their parents answered. "Keep your eyes open,
you just might see her!"

The children of River John were ever on the alert, always playing a bit of hide and seek, looking out for woolly treasures and a chance sighting of old Polly MacCauley. And because they were a little afraid of her, they had rude and silly games that made fun of her.

Polly MacCauley's in the barn!
She'll lasso you with magical yarn.
She'll hook your heart to a wagon cart!
She'll feed you boogers and farty tarts.
She'll shear your head until you're dead,
So scram like a lamb, run while you can!
Run, run faster than the gingerbread man!

Honestly, the things some people dream up.
This is a yarn, so decide for yourself if all this is true—
but one thing's for sure—sure enough, Polly MacCauley heard baby
lamb's first few BAAAAS!

"Woolly and wild or meek and mild, hurrah, a new baby lamb is born!"
she squeaked in her rusty dusty voice.
She opened the window and breathed in.
SNNNIFF!

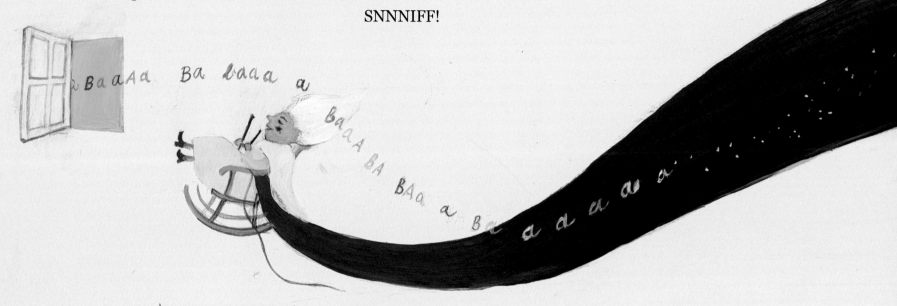

She took another big whiff of the sweet lilac breeze.
SNIFFFF!
Then she plunked her squeaky creaky bones back down and rocked
in her squeaky creaky rocking chair faster than she had rocked
in a very squeaky creaky long time.

"Yes!
Soon I'll have the yarn I need to finish what I began so long ago.
    Clickety clack Clickety click,
Clickety clickety clickety click—
    back and forth,
row after row,
    I knit and I sit, I sit and I knit.
Thank you, sweet lamb,
    my new baby lambie!
I'll knit socks and mittens and slippers; I'll felt and weave and hook,
    but now I knooooooow, hey ho hey hooooooooo,
I'll knit from your wool
my very finest,
most divinest,
woolliest gift of all!"

Buddy had been right, you see. Polly MacCauley really was getting very near the end
of her yarn, and had been

waiting,

waiting,

waiting for this lamb to be born.

For a very long time, she had been working on what she considered her masterpiece.
And this masterpiece required a special kind of wool
from a special baby lamb.

3

Meanwhile back at the barn, things weren't all
hunky dory, sweetness and light, happy honeybee
humming along.

              Not at all.

Baby Lamb was fine, but her mother was not.
One night, about a month after the birth, as the moon
rose over the red-roofed farmhouse, as star fires lit up
the night sky, the baby lamb's mother bleated
      one last loving *baa* to her baby lamb
and then?

Well, yes, I'm sad to say,
       she
         died.

At that very moment, Polly MacCauley's knitting needles stopped their clickety clack.
Even without being there, Polly MacCauley knew exactly what had happened.
"Poor lambie," she sighed, and looked up at the moon.

The sound of Baby Lamb's sad cries vibrated all along the Sunrise Trail—
from River John west to Tatamagouche,
to Wallace and Pugwash and Amherst,
from River John northeast to Pictou.
Such wails that made everyone's hearts just about burst.
From New Glasgow to Merigomish and Antigonish to the Cabot Trail—
news of the loss of that mother travelled far.
Those cries could be heard right across the Cabot Strait
to the island of Newfoundland, up through the Codroy Valley,
to Deer Lake and Gander and Kelligrews,
all the way to Witless Bay and Mobile and Tors Cove,
where the sheep on Ship Island heard them and baaaed baaaack.

All the way to the Big Dipper and Jupiter and London and New York and Tokyo, too.
To the savannas of Africa, the snow-capped tips of the Himalayan Mountains
and the ice floes in the Northwest Passage of the Arctic Ocean.

And anywhere else you'd like to guess or imagine. Paris?
    Oui! oui!
        Ecum Secum?
            Wherever your imagination takes you.

A tale can't be tall if you keep dreaming small.

And yes indeed,
        Count Woolliam and his sister,
            the Countess of Fleece and Fluff,
                also heard those sorrowful cries.

"An orphaned lamb? All the better! Without a mother—that lamb is ours for the taking!"

And on they sailed through seas of fluffy stuff and woolly storms, following wavy strands of yarn. They passed pods of porpoises, and gazed at the gulp of cormorants overhead. And the bleating baas of that baby lamb grew stronger and stronger.

"Perhaps our journey will be long," Count Woolliam said to the Countess of Fleece and Fluff, "but soon we will have that lamb!"

"And we will be rich *rich* **rich**," laughed Woolamina.

"And always warm, and never cold!"

Meanwhile, out on deck, their helpers were freezing as they slopped the deck and steered the ship and cooked the meals and tended the sheep.

It was all "Yes, Your Woolness" and "No, Your Woolness" and "Right away, Your Woolness."

 **4**

Baaa,

       baa,

             baaaaaa.

For many days Baby Lamb cried out for her mother.

    Baa Baa baabaa baa ba baa, answered the sheep of the North Shore in Sheep Speak.

In Gaelic, this means "tha sinn duilich airson do chall."

    In Mi'kmaq, this means "meskeyi."

In French, this means "nous sommes désolées pour votre deuil."

    In English, this means "we are sorry for your loss."

So, yes, death happens—even on the Sunrise Trail.

There is such sadness when we lose someone we love, but perhaps
you yourself have noticed that both people and sheep can be extra kind
in hard and sorrowful times.

We may cry tears for different reasons,
But everyone knows deep sorrowful seasons.

Farmer John and Farmer Gillian and their son Rory and their daughter Katy
took extra *extra* **extra** special care of Baby Lamb.

But Baby Lamb still cried and grew thin.
They took turns bottle-feeding and petting her.
Still, she would not eat.
Farmer John sang a song in Gaelic.

> *Muile nam fuar bheann, Mòrbhairn' an àigh,*
> *Apainn na grèine 's Latharn' mo ghràidh...*

Farmer Gillian washed Baby Lamb's face and brushed her fleece.
Rory and Katy sat by her side.
Still that little lamb cried. And cried. And cried.

> But...

When Polly MacCauley heard those cries,
she kissed three of her favourite hummingbirds,
then opened her window.

The hummingbirds fluttered off and landed on the tippety-tip of Baby Lamb's nose.
 If you've never had a hummingbird's kiss, it's soft as fleece, and just as tickle-ish.
And it can cure whatever ails you.

Soon, Baby Lamb was finishing the bottles Katy fed her in greedy gulp time.
One day, finally, she wobbled, and she stood up.

"YES!" said Katy. "YES!" She decided she must name the wee lamb right away.

"Your name is Star because you were born when the waves were
sparkly, and because your mother died on such a starry night.
And because you will shine brightly!"

"Baaa Baa," bleated Star.
To Katy, it sounded like "thank you."

Some days, Star was a gamboling lamb; she danced and kicked up her heels
in the pastures of Lismore Sheep Farm. Some days, Star was a glum lump of a lamb;
she grumbled and mumbled and moped. Even though Star had lots of cousins
and a few great aunts, when she watched the other baby lambs snuggle
onto their mothers' backs and fall asleep, night after night,
she wished she had a mother of her own.

Star could've been and would've been one sad and lonely sheep at bedtime,
bleating herself to sleep. But an old sheep that everyone called
Grammy Lamb comforted her every night
with bedtime stories and lullabies.

"Tell me a story, that story of where I come from again,"
  Star pleaded every night.

"Well, you've heard of the ship *Hector*, that ship
  that landed in Pictou?"

"Yes, indeed we have," bleated all the sheep in the barn.
"Many times."

"Well, Star, your kin came over on the ship *Polly* from Potrie in the Isle of Skye,
not far from Lismore that this farm's named after, and some stayed across the strait
in Prince Edward Island, and some crossed over here to New Scotland. But the thing
you need know is your kin's seen rough times and sad times—leaving one's home is never
easy, but home travels with you wherever you end up. Now, if I remember what my
mother told me the ship *Polly* was no ordinary ship ...... there was magic on board ..."

And Grammy Lamb would continue on and on and on, and even sang a lullaby
or three or four. And before too long, Star was rocked to sleep, rocked as if she was
on a ship herself, that one that sails on a sea of sound and syllables and song and story.

Time passed, as time does, and after a spell (from Polly MacCauley, no doubt),
what with all that love and attention, Star grew sturdy; her eyes clear
and bright with curiosity.

As everyone knows, curiosity is a sign of intelligence.

"She's a special one, all right," said Farmer John.

"All the lambs are special," Katy reminded her father.

"Indeed," said Farmer John, "but this one, well, *this* one has something extra-special.
I feel it in my bones. She **is** a Star."

But every day, as
the farmers were plowing
        the fisherfolk fishing
    the fiddlers were fiddling
    the bakers were baking
  the makers were making
the preachers were praying
          the readers were reading
      the children were playing
    the hens were laying
   the gardeners were sowing
  the carpenters sawing
 the chickadees chirping
the babies were burping
the crows were cawing
the roosters were crowing
the mowers were mowing
the green grass was growing
      and .....
  an uncommonly lovely
    lucky lilac-
      lavender breeze
        was *blooooow*-ing—

Star did not feel especially special
in any special way.
She did not know what
she was supposed to ... **do**.

I don't
plow like farmers
fish like fisherfolk
fiddle like fiddlers   bake like bakers
make like makers
pray like preachers   read like readers
play like children   lay like hens
sow like gardeners
saw like carpenters
chirp like chickadees   burp like babies
caw like crows   crow like roosters
mow like mowers
grow like grass, and.....

CAW
CAW CAW

CAW   CAW

B BAA a a a baa BAA A A A

I
don't
feel
lucky!

  (And she didn't smell like lilac or lavender at all!)

Furthermore,
I don't
    meow like a cat
bark like a dog   oink like a pig
    leap like a frog
            make honey like the bees
moo like a cow   spin like a spider
I just don't know how.

"I'm a lamb, I am," she said. "And that's all I am."
And somehow, it did not seem enough.
A lamb without a mother, and a lamb without a purpose.
"Sure, I'm 'special.' I'm just eSpecially good fer **nothing**."

But little did Star know,
every day as Polly MacCauley sat down to knit she said:
"Clickety clack Clickety click,
Clickety clickety clickety click—
back and forth,
row after row,
I knit and sit, I sit and knit.
Thank you, sweet sheep,
my wee little lambies!
I'll knit socks and mittens and slippers and shawls,
And I'll knit from your wool my very finest,
most divinest,
woolliest gift of all."

And it was right strange—the sound of Polly MacCauley's
knitting needles could be heard throughout the village.

But she was still rather lonely.
And a wee bit worried.
She was also almost out of yarn.

And, little did Star know, that at exactly that very same moment in time, a noble search party from the county of Woolland was crossing an ocean, on its way to find her.

"We must be the ones who capture her ourselves," said Count Woolliam to his sister Woolamina, the Countess of Fleece and Fluff. "Then the lamb will do whatever we command. We will be **woollionaires** forever."

Woollionaires are people who are stinking rich and have more skeins of wool than they know what to do with. BUT
    The more skeins they gain, they more they want,
    And the more there is to get tangled and twisted!

Now, here is where our own yarn becomes a bit tangled and twisted.

Polly MacCauley knew that the time for Star's first shearing was fast approaching.

And she knew that Star's fleece would make the wool she needed
to finish her *very finest, most divinest, woolliest gift of all.*

So on a morning when sunlight spread like melted butter across an ink-blue sky,
Polly MacCauley mustered all her courage, and for the first time in many years,
in **broaaad** daylight, she left her little house in the middle of the woods.

She trudged across the iron bridge that crossed the John River.
She stopped in the middle of the bridge, took a deep sniff
of the uncommonly lovely lucky lilac-lavender breeze.

She remembered long-ago summers when, as a child, she'd splashed into the water,
swinging from the rope below. She waved to the children who were doing that very thing.

"Is it? Could it **be**? Polly MacCauley!!!" they screamed. Then they chanted:
  She'll hitch your heart to a wagon cart and feed you boogers and farty tarts.

Polly MacCauley just smiled, and continued on her way, tramping through the trail
in the woods, hoping no bears or wolves were close by.

Finally the woods thinned and the trail ended at the Legion by the village's edge.
She paused and remembered the long-past wars, and the soldiers who had gone far away
to fight, and the young soldier she was supposed to marry.
David Douglas Dougal MacDonald, his name was.
  So many pairs of socks she'd knit for him. So many letters she'd written.
    But when David Douglas Dougal MacDonald finally came home to River John,
      he came home in a coffin.
        There was a funeral in the village instead of a wedding.

Polly MacCauley walked on, a sadness in her heart
heavier than a wet woollen blanket.

Polly MacCauley wiped her eyes with her handkerchief
and a hummingbird kissed the tip of her nose and her sadness lifted,
and so she *bashed on regardless*:
  through the village,
    past the library,
      the pharmacy,
        the fire hall,
          and the building where the school used to be,
            past the post office and a church.

And when the whole village realized this was the one and only Polly MacCauley—

the farmers stopped plowing   the fisherfolk stopped fishing
    the fiddlers stopped fiddling
the bakers stopped baking   the makers stopped making
the preachers stopped praying   the readers stopped reading
    the children stopped playing   the hens stopped laying
the gardeners stopped sowing   the carpenters stopped sawing
    the chickadees stopped chirping
the babies stopped burping   the crows stopped cawing
    the roosters stopped crowing   the mowers stopped mowing
the green grass stopped growing

and ....
    the breeze grew
        uncommonly
          still.

Every living creature that could, followed Polly MacCauley as she strode bravely up Bill's Hill, turned onto Louisville Road and hupp hupped up the long driveway that led to Lismore Sheep Farm.

She knocked on the door of the wool shop with a knockety knock knock sound, very like the clickety click click of her knitting needles.

"Good golly! It's Polly MacCauley," said Farmer Gillian and Farmer John. "Finally!" "We've been waiting for you forever!"

"You have?" exclaimed Polly MacCauley.

"If you pass the test, Star is yours."

"TEST? I'm not very good at tests..." she began.

"Come to the barn! This one is easy, and it's not about you!"

"Looks like the whole village is here," said Rory.
He turned to the crowd,
"Only Polly's allowed inside!"

The barn smelled sweetly of fresh hay and was filled
with the bleating of many sheep.

Polly MacCauley entered.

Star lifted her head and saw Polly.

BAAAAA! BAAAA. She bleated. And then?

Star leapt over five sheep, three bales of hay, two wooden gates
and jumped right up in Polly MacCauley's arms.

BaaaBAa.

Now as I was told the tale, it was said
that Star actually said MAAAAaMAAAA.

But if you stretch a yarn too tight and thin,
it breaks apart, gets harder to spin.

(So whatever really happened, here's what happened next.)

Polly MacCauley was overjoyed!

"My sweet lambie, I'll knit from your wool my very finest, most divinest, woolliest gift of all."

"Yep, she's yours alright."

"We wouldn't give this special lamb to just anybody," said Katy.
"And I have to be able to come visit, okay?"

"I'll get some things together," said Rory.

"Not so fast. Not so fast!" A commanding voice echoed throughout the barn.

And there, standing in the door of the barn, were Count Woolliam and the Countess Woolamina, surrounded by their search party and the crowd of villagers.

Baaa A a

"Announcing," shouted Woolliam in a loud and strange voice,
"their Noble Woolnesses, Count Woolliam and Woolamina, the Countess of Fleece
and Fluff, from the county of Woolland. They have travelled from far away
to come for the lamb whose sorrowful cries they have followed here."

"We shall take her for our own," Woolliam continued, in his own voice. "As she has
no mother, she belongs in our county where she will provide wool for our countship."

Farmers John and Gillian, and Katy and Rory looked at each other. Polly MacCauley
began to tremble. How could she compete for ownership of Star with the likes
of Count Woolliam and the Countess of Fleece and Fluff?

"As a courtesy, we will pay you the handsome sum of five of our pure bred sheep,"
said Count Woolliam, as five old and straggly sheep were herded forward. "Here.
Take them, and we'll be on our way."

The villagers shouted: "No! no! No! This lamb is our lamb, not yours to take."
Voices of the villagers echoed in the fields.

"She is already spoken for," said Polly quietly, in her rusty dusty voice.

Farmer John and Farmer Gillian folded their arms and stood in front of Star.
Katy and Rory folded their arms and stood in front of Farmer John and Farmer Gillian.

The Count and Countess looked at the villagers outside the door, and they looked
at Farmers John and Gillian, and they looked at Katy and Rory and Polly,
standing there by Star. And they began whispering furiously to each other.

"We will be back to get Star in the morning," said Count Woolliam. "At day break.
Unless, of course, you convince us otherwise!!!!"

"Not!" laughed the Countess, then she tried very hard to sound sincere.
"But you can try. Effort is always commendable."

They left quickly, with their eyes on the ground,
their hands over their ears, and their hearts squeezed shut
so they did not have to listen to what everyone was saying.

As soon as they were gone, Buddy, who was standing
with all the fellows from Yap's, cleared his throat and said: "Village huddle time!"

Soon dozens of voices were calling out:
      "We have lost our bank and lost our grocery store."
          "We've lost our school; we have lost many friends."
        "Many have lost money."
            "And some of us have lost faith."

Then one rusty dusty voice rang out above them all:
      "But we must not lose our way! We will not lose this lamb!"

Even though not everyone in the village always saw eye to eye, and they had
to agree to disagree over many things, in this instant, on this night, they all agreed.

            Star MUST stay.

They worked through the night, on and on until sunrise—and that morning the sunrise on the Sunrise Trail was simply spectacular.

And by the time that simply spectacular sunrise had peeked into the barn, they had come up with a plan.

And, when the Count and Countess showed up?

Here's what happened.

"We think we have found a way to convince you," said Polly MacCauley.

"Really?" said the Count, and he rolled his eyes.

"Ain't this quaint," said the Countess. "Whoppedy do."

"Coffee first?" offered Farmer Gillian.

"Here, why not try a pastry," said Polly, and she passed them a plate of farty tarts. She'd baked them herself and hoped they would sweeten the Count and the Countess up just a little.

The farmers said, "We'll give you vegetables to take back to your land."

The fisherfolk said, "We'll give you lobster instead of our lamb."

The fiddlers fiddled a brand new tune, the Woolland Waltz, just for them.

The bakers said, "We'll bake you a loaf!"

The makers said, "We'll make you mittens."

The preachers said, "We'll send you our prayers."

The readers said, "We will read you a story."

The children said, "We'll sing you a song."

The hens produced green eggs.

The gardeners said, "We will share our seeds."

The carpenters said, "We'll build you a mansion."

The chickadees chirped a symphony.

The babies only pooped and peed.

The crows cawed in loud applause.

The roosters cock-a-doodle-doo-ed. The mowers did a dance with scythes.

 The green grass glowed through that countryside,
and ...

the breeze grew
uncommonly
still.

"Wool, I never!" cranked Count Woolliam. "Ingrates!"

But Countess Woolamina was weeping. "We lost our mother when we were young,
and no one since has loved us like this village loves this lamb."

"Your nobleness," said Polly MacCauley. "This lamb is royalty to all of us.
She is Star of the Sunrise Trail, and this is the place where she belongs.
If she were to leave her home, her fleece will never be the same.
And I need that fleece to create
    my finest,
        most divinest,
            woolliest gift of all."

COCK-a-DOODLe-DOO-eD

The Count looked at Polly MacCauley. He looked at Star.
He looked at the people from the village, and then
at his sister. He sniffled a little, too.

He was flooded with a warmth he had never felt before.
Something, some hole in his greedy brittle heart, stitched together.

"Yes," said Count Woolliam. "Home in River John is where
Star belongs. I am so pleased to have met you all AND
such a fine lamb as well. I hope Star will keep many, many warm."

Ba a a A A BA

Then their Noble Woolnesses left, blowing kisses
from their woolly, woolly mittens.

The next morning when Star woke up in Polly MacCauley's barn,
which was really a house fit for a Lamb, she felt ALIVE!

B A A A !

"Star! Just as I hoped. Just as I knew!" said Polly MacCauley.
Star had grown a very thick coat of fleece.
Whizz whirr buzz done! Polly sheared the fleece from Star.
Miracles of miracles, in just one night, Star grew another new beautiful fleece!
And the next day, and the day after that,
        and all the days that followed—the same thing happened.
Soon all Polly had to do was take her knitting needles to the barn
        and knit from Star's fleece.
Star was happier than she had ever been.
        She had a mama and a purpose.
And Polly MacCauley began work
        again on her masterpiece.

Then, one morning, a group of women knocked on her door.

"Polly MacCauley, you need company," they said. "And helpers.
Because we are better when we are together."

Well, Polly couldn't tell them about Star's magic fleece,
but she had a lot of yarn saved up. "Come on in," she said.

They bustled right in her door and arranged chairs and formed a circle.
They made pots and pots of elderberry tea
and nibbled Mrs. MacGregor's Scotch cookies
and Polly MacCauley's farty tarts with radish relish
(which were actually delicious)
and they knit.

And they knit.

And they knit.

At first they made little sweaters and hats for all the newborn babies in the village.
Then they made mittens for all the children in River John.
    Then they made socks for the fishermen
and scarves for everyone on the Sunrise Trail.
    Scarves of blue like the blue of the sea.
Scarves of red and orange like the red of lobsters and the orange of campfires.
    Scarves of yellow like the rising sun.
Scarves of pink for the evening sky.
    Scarves of purple for the lavender fields.
Scarves of green like the green of the meadows along that Sunrise Trail.

They hooked, they felted, they wove wondrous creations, and finally, these creations
went all around the world to keep children and grownups warm in far-off lands.
Useful things. Beautiful things.
All from the wool of one little lamb.

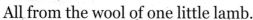

There was lots of yarn.

Always lots of yarn.

This was something Count Woolliam and Countess Woolamina had come to understand.
Like love, there is always enough wool to go around. And they travelled the world making
sure everyone had enough of both.

So Star kept sharing, and Polly kept shearing, and others kept carding and spinning
and weaving and hooking and felting and knitting.

Polly MacCauley wasn't so lonely anymore.

And at night by the light of the moon,

she knit clickety click on her masterpiece.

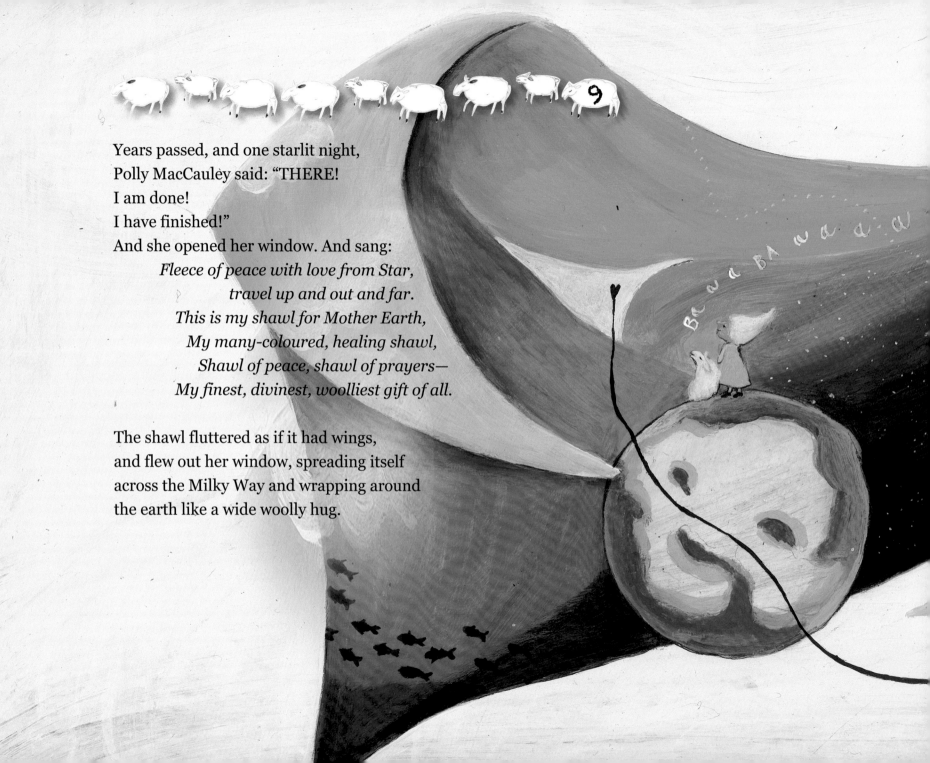

Years passed, and one starlit night,
Polly MacCauley said: "THERE!
I am done!
I have finished!"
And she opened her window. And sang:
> *Fleece of peace with love from Star,*
> *travel up and out and far.*
> *This is my shawl for Mother Earth,*
> *My many-coloured, healing shawl,*
> *Shawl of peace, shawl of prayers—*
> *My finest, divinest, woolliest gift of all.*

The shawl fluttered as if it had wings,
and flew out her window, spreading itself
across the Milky Way and wrapping around
the earth like a wide woolly hug.

Then Polly MacCauley took her needles
and went into the barn.

"Star, you have been such a friend.
You have warmed the days and nights,
and have made my heart glad. Thanks
to you, my masterpiece is finished
and my time has come."

With that, her knitting needles stopped
their clickety click,
and her kind old heart stopped
its tickety tick.

Star's sad bleating travelled far.

She went back to Lismore Sheep Farm, and once again she was taken care of by Farmer John and Farmer Gillian, and by Rory and Katy.

When the village buried Polly MacCauley beside David Douglas Dougal MacDonald,

the bagpipers were piping
the highland dancers were flinging
the fiddlers were fiddling
the children were singing
the weavers were weaving
the spinners were spinning,
even the curmudgeonly curmudgeons
were grinning.

Baaaa Baaa

The village was dressed
in its village best, awaiting
The Noble Guests:

yes, Count Woolliam and Woolamina returned to River John to attend the service.
They brought Star a present—a very handsome sheep.

"I'm a Ram, I am," bleated the sheep.
"I woolly woolly love you, Star."

Now, it is said that Polly MacCauley's finest, divinest, woolliest gift of all,
that shawl of healing and hope, is so beautiful and so dazzling, it is hard to look upon,
and sometimes, because it is so hard to see, people forget it is there.

But I'm here to tell you that I know it is because I have felt its warmth and healing.

Once, long ago, Polly MacCauley asked me to spin this yarn
when she was gone. So now I have,
and I gave my yarn to a friend because:

Everyone's tangled together
in a beautiful design—
My heart is yours and yours is mine.

Imagine this:

A lamb named Star is getting ready to have a baby,
And somewhere far way, a man sleeping outside on a bench
    wakes up to find warm socks;
A woman who was sick and lost her hair is wearing a felted hat
    and feels strong again;
And children who had none are snuggled under
    a blanket and dreaming.

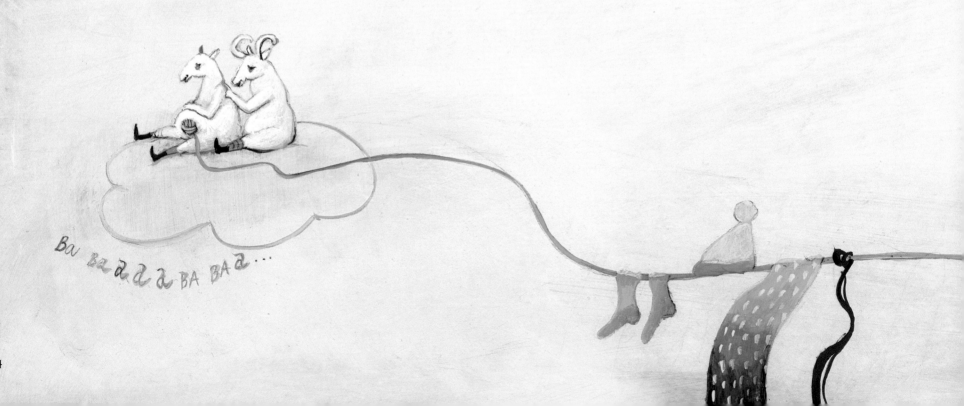

Ba Ba a a a BA BA a ...

Wherever and whenever someone needs a bit of wool
or a bit of warmth or maybe the piecing together of a sad
and lonely heart, perhaps they might see the tail of a scarf,
like a whisper of hope, blowing around the next corner,
or they might look up and wrap themselves up
in the power of Polly MacCauley's finest, divinest,
woolliest gift of all.

"Tales are for telling and the truth may be tall,
My yarn is for spinning as the earth spins for all."

THE End

of my yarn is the beginning of your spinning ....

Star still lives with her family on the Sunrise Trail.

Thanks to many shepherds in my life: the Crawfords, my first friends in River John; John Crawford, for leading me to the Lismore song; Susan MacConnell, for leading me to the ship *Polly*; David Baxter and Deb Plestid, friends, artists, and makers extraordinaire; Deanne Fitzpatrick, for sisterhood and magic in her studio; the River John Square knitters, for their work and inspiration; Shar MacLean, who led me to Bill's Hill; Valrie Suidgeest, for leading by example and local tidbits; the River John Legion, where history is cherished, stories told, and suppers served; exquisite artists Marnie and Darka and Veselina, for their sense of beauty, for caring about every syllable and line and curve; the friends I've found along the North Shore of Nova Scotia, River John, and Pictou County, where we've discovered community with a spirit of resilience that can never be taken away. Blessed to have Rev. Nicole Uzans, Sister Rebecca Mckenna, and Jan Watson in my life—women of wisdom who offer words that lead me by still waters. As ever, to my deeply dimpled darling Gilles, who led me to River John to begin with, who fixes and heals and makes the world more beautiful and me more useful beyond and—in spite of—my wildest imaginings. Finally, to every lamb, four legged and otherwise, whose every bleat is code for: I'm hungry or ... I just woolly woolly love you.
~ Sheree Fitch

Thanks to my family and friends.
~ Darka Erdelji

Running the Goat thanks Margaret Bennett for help with Gaelic, Amelia Reimer and Curtis Michael for help with Mi'kmaq, Claire Wilkshire for help with French, and Anne Crawford Major for taking a look.

On page 30, Farmer John sings the chorus of "Fàgail Lios Mòr" ("Leaving Lismore") to Star.

The typeface is Georgia, which was designed by Matthew Carter.
It has been chosen for use in this book as an homage
to the publisher's mother, Georgia Parsons,
who has spent a long and generous life knitting and weaving beautiful things
for family and friends, and in support of her community's hospital auxiliary.
Like Polly, she offers wool and warmth to the world.

This book was designed by Veselina Tomova
of Vis-à-Vis Graphics,
St. John's, Newfoundland and Labrador,
and printed by Friesens in Canada.

978-1-927917-10-7

Running the Goat
Books & Broadsides Inc.
54 Cove Road
Tors Cove, Newfoundland and Labrador A0A 4A0
www.runningthegoat.com